This book belongs to

_____

NurseryRhymes

Kate Toms

make
believe
ideas

This little piggy

This little piggy
went to market.
This little piggy
stayed at home.
This little piggy
had roast beef.
This little piggy
had none.
And this little
piggy cried,
"Wee, wee, wee!"
all the way home.

Wee wee Wee

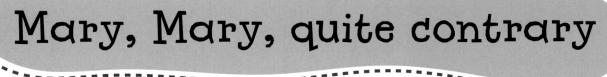

Mary, Mary, quite contrary

Mary, Mary,
quite contrary,
how does your
garden grow?
With silver bells
and cockle shells,
and pretty maids
all in a row.

Pat-a-cake, pat-a-cake

yummy

Pat-a-cake, pat-a-cake,
baker's man,
bake me a cake
as fast as you can.
Pat it and prick it
and mark it with B,
put it in the oven
for Baby and me.

Row, row, row your boat

Row, row, row your boat
gently down the stream;
merrily, merrily, merrily, merrily,
life is but a dream.

Row, row, row your boat
gently on the tide;
merrily, merrily, merrily, merrily,
to the other side.

Row, row, row your boat
gently back to shore;
merrily, merrily, merrily, merrily,
home for tea at four.

The other side welcomes you

Mulberry Bush

Here we go round the Mulberry Bush,
the Mulberry Bush, the Mulberry Bush.
Here we go round the Mulberry Bush
on a cold and frosty morning.

This is the way we clap our hands,
clap our hands, clap our hands.
This is the way we clap our hands
on a cold and frosty morning.

This is the way we stamp our feet,
stamp our feet, stamp our feet.
This is the way we stamp our feet
on a cold and frosty morning.

Jump up and down!

Clap our hands!

Stamp our feet!

One potato, two potato

One potato, two potato,
three potato, four.
Five potato, six potato,
seven potato, more!
Eight potato, nine potato,
ten potato high.
Now let's go and bake
some sweet potato pie!

Baa, baa, black sheep

Baa, baa, black sheep,
have you any wool?
Yes sir, yes sir,
three bags full.
One for the master,
one for the dame,
one for the little boy
who lives down the lane.

Sing a song of sixpence

Sing a song of sixpence,
a pocket full of rye,
four and twenty blackbirds
baked in a pie.
When the pie was opened,
the birds began to sing,
oh, wasn't that a dainty dish
to set before the king?

The king was in his counting-house,
counting out his money,
the queen was in the parlour,
eating bread and honey,
the maid was in the garden,
hanging out the clothes,
when down came a blackbird
and pecked off her nose!

Tra la la!

That's not funny!

Humpty Dumpty

Humpty Dumpty
sat on a wall,
Humpty Dumpty
had a great fall.
All the king's horses
and all the king's men
couldn't put Humpty
together again.

Sorry about that!

Jack and Jill

Jack and Jill went up the hill
to fetch a pail of water.
Jack fell down and broke his crown
and Jill came tumbling after.

Up Jack got and home did trot
as fast as he could caper;
and went to bed to mend his head
with vinegar and brown paper.

Oh noooo!

Hickory dickory dock

Hickory dickory dock,
the mouse ran up the clock.
The clock struck one,
the mouse ran down,
hickory dickory dock.

tick tock

tick tock

Bong!

Incy Wincy Spider

Incy Wincy Spider
climbed up the water spout.
Down came the rain
and washed poor Incy out.

Out came the sunshine
and dried up all the rain,
and Incy Wincy Spider
climbed up the spout again.

Here I go again!

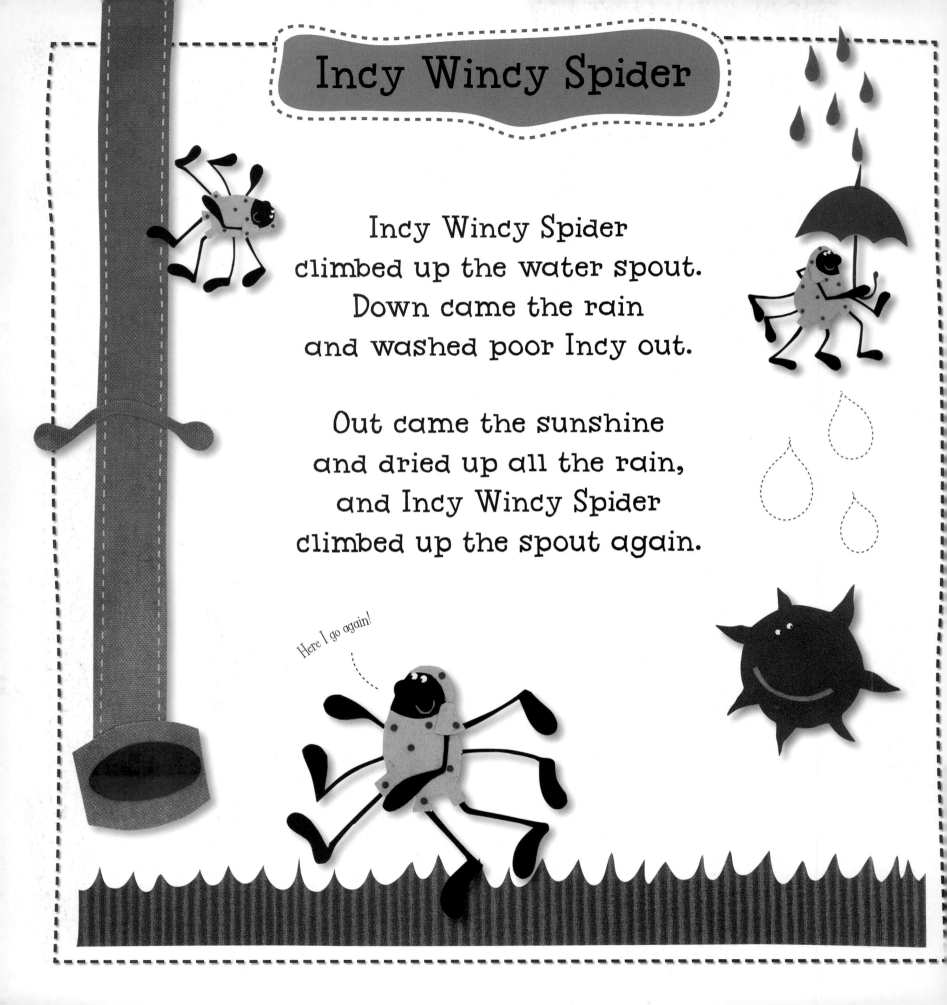

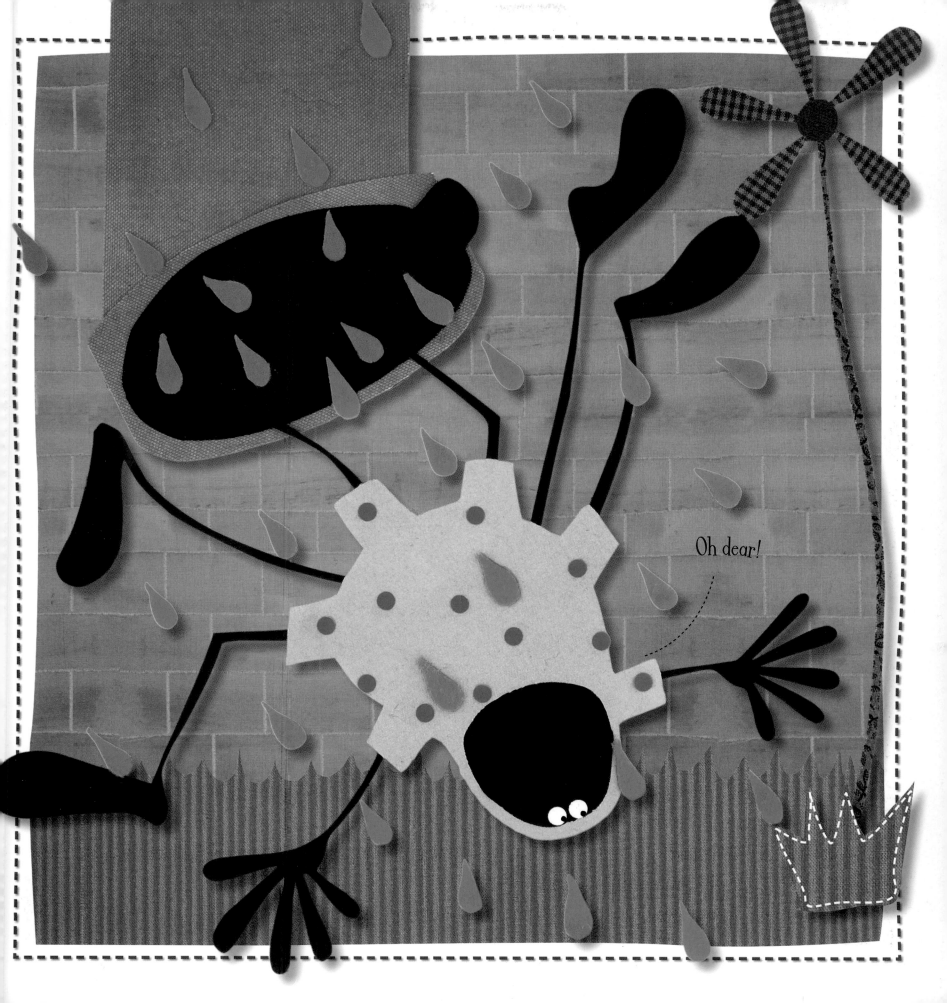

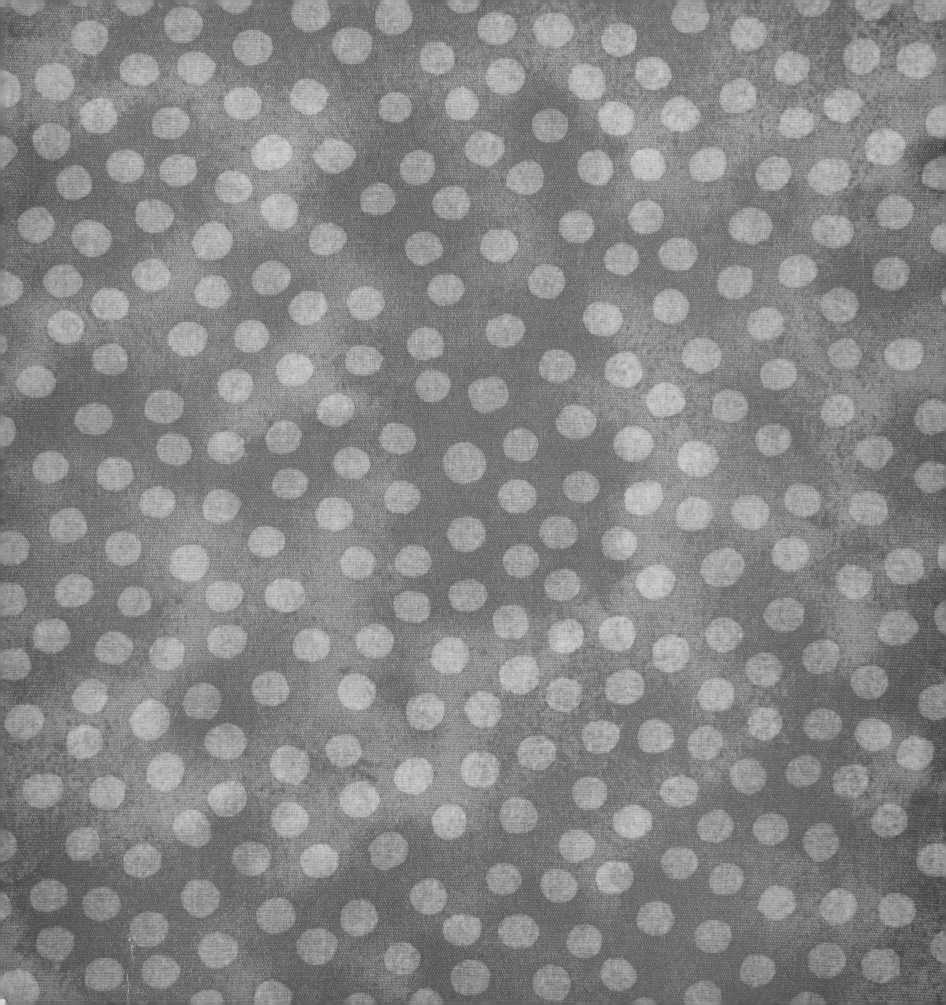